Mister Pip

For Pip, my prince.

Mister Pip

Thereza Rowe

Tate Publishing

Here comes Mister Pip.

Always ready for his dinner.

MUNCH
CRUNCH
MUNCH

Then to find a quiet spot to sleep.

Unfortunately, it's not too long before ...

VROOOM

... a monster startles.

RING,
RING

The bug wakes up.

RUMBLE, RUMBLE

An earthquake strikes.

Not a hint of trouble, until ...

WEEWOOO

... daylight robbery disturbs.

A diva makes a scene.

Messy eaters ...

PLOFT!

... and pesky canoodlers annoy.

COO
COO

At last! The perfect spot, until ...

KABOOM

the sky roars.

A curious cushion appeals.

'Mister Pip, look out!'

SSSSS

SSHHHH

Finally, Mister Pip falls ...

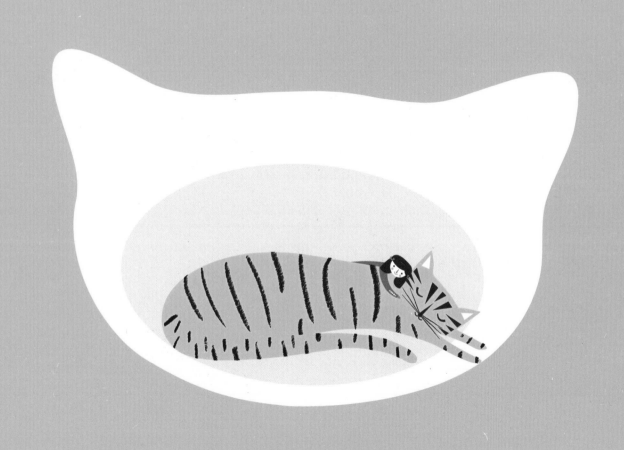

... sound asleep.

Just as well he's had a good nap.

As dusk arrives, here comes Mister Pip.

Ready for his dinner ...

... and plenty of fun.

'Good night Mister Pip!'

First published 2016 by order of the Tate Trustees
by Tate Publishing, a division of Tate Enterprises Ltd,
Millbank, London SW1P 4RG
www.tate.org.uk/publishing

A catalogue record for this book is available from the British Library
ISBN 978 1 84976 382 0

Distributed in the United States and Canada by ABRAMS, New York

Library of Congress Control Number applied for

Designed by Dominika Lipniewska
Colour reproduction by Evergreen Colour Management Ltd, Hong Kong

Printed and bound in China by Toppan Leefung Printing Ltd